ALSO BY CAROLINE M. YOACHIM

Seven Wonders of a Once and Future World

THE
ARCHRONOLOGY
OF LOVE

THE
ARCHRONOLOGY
OF LOVE

CAROLINE M.
YOACHIM

FAIRWOOD PRESS
Bonney Lake, WA

THE ARCHRONOLOGY OF LOVE
A Fairwood Press Book
Copyright © 2019
by Caroline M. Yoachim

Fairwood Press
21528 104th Street Ct E
Bonney Lake WA 98391

See all our titles at:
www.fairwoodpress.com

"The Archronology of Love"
originally appeared at *Lightspeed* © 2019

"Flowers in the Chronicle"
appears here for the first time © 2020

ISBN: 978-1-933846-96-5

Fairwood Press First Edition:
March 2020

Cover image © 2019 by Reiko Murakami
Cover and book design by Patrick Swenson

Printed in the United States of America

To my lifelove

CONTENTS

THE
ARCHRONOLOGY
OF LOVE

This is a love story, the last of a series of moments when we meet.

Saki Jones leaned into the viewport until her nose nearly touched the glass, staring at the colony planet below. New Mars. From this distance, she could pretend that things were going according to plan—that M.J. was waiting for her in one of the domed cities. A shuttle would take her down to the surface and she and her lifelove would pursue their dream of studying a grand alien civilization.

It had been such a beautiful plan.

"Dr. Jones?" The crewhand at the entrance to the observation deck was an elderly white woman, part of the skeleton team that had worked long shifts in empty space while the passengers had slept in stasis. "The captain has requested an accelerated schedule on your research. She sent you the details? All our surface probes have malfunctioned, and she needs you to look at the time record of the colony collapse."

"The Chronicle." Saki corrected the woman automatically, most of her attention still on the planet below. "The time record is called the Chronicle."

"Right. The captain—"

Saki turned away from the viewport. "Sorry. I have the captain's message. Please reassure her that I will gather my team and get research underway as soon as possible."

The woman saluted and left. Saki sent a message calling the department together for an emergency meeting and returned to the viewport. New Mars was the same angry red as its namesake, and the colony cities looked like pus-filled boils on its surface. It was a dangerous place—malevolent and sick. M.J. had died there. If they hadn't been too broke to go together, the whole family would have died. Saki blinked away tears. She had to stay focused.

It was a violation of protocol for Saki to go into the Chronicle. No one was ever a truly impartial observer, of course, but she'd had M.J. torn away so suddenly, so unexpectedly. The pain of it was raw and overwhelming. They'd studied together, raised children together, planned an escape from Earth. Other partners had come and gone from their lives, but she and M.J. had always been there for each other.

If she went into the Chronicle, she would look for him. It would bias her choices and her observations. But she *was* the most qualified person on the team, and if she recused herself she could lose her research grant, her standing in the department, her dream of studying alien civilizations . . . and her chance to see M.J.

"Dr. Jones . . ." A softer voice this time—one of her graduate students. Hyun-sik was immaculately dressed, as always, with shimmery blue eyeliner that matched his blazer.

"I know, Hyun-sik. The projector is

ready and we're on an accelerated schedule. I just need a few moments to gather my thoughts before the site-selection meeting."

"That's not why I'm here," Hyun-sik said. "I didn't mean to intrude, but I wanted to offer my support. My parents were also at the colony. Whatever happened down there is a great loss to all of us."

Saki didn't know what to say. Words always felt so meaningless in the face of death. She and Hyun-sik hadn't spoken much about their losses during the months of deceleration after they woke from stasis. They'd thrown themselves into their research, used their work as a distraction from their pain. "Arriving at the planet re-opened a lot of wounds."

"I sent my parents ahead because I thought their lives would be better here than back on Earth." He gestured at the viewport. "The temptation to see them again is strong. So close, and the Chronicle is right there. I know you're struggling with the same dilemma. It must be a difficult decision for you, having lost M.J.—"

"Yes." Saki interrupted before Hyun-sik could say anything more. Even hearing M.J.'s name was difficult. She was unfit for this expedition. She should take a leave of absence and allow Li Yingtai take over as lead. But this research was her dream, their dream—M.J.'s and hers—and these were unusual circumstances. Saki frowned. "How did you know I was here, thinking about recusing myself?"

"It isn't difficult to guess. It's what I would be doing, in your place." He looked away. "But also Kenzou told me at our lunch date today."

Saki sighed. Her youngest son was the only one of her children who had opted to leave Earth and come with her. He'd thought that New Mars would be a place of adventure and opportunity. Silly romantic notions. For the last few weeks she'd barely seen him—he'd mentioned having a new boyfriend but hadn't talked about the details. She'd been concerned because the relationship had drawn him away from his studies. Pilots weren't in high demand now, he'd said, given the state of the colony. Apparently his mystery boyfriend was her smart, attractive, six-years-older-than-Kenzou graduate student. She was disappointed to find out about the relationship from her student rather than her son. He was drifting away from her, and she didn't know how to mend the rift.

Hyun-sik wrung his hands, clearly ill at ease with the new turn in the conversation.

"I think you and Kenzou make a lovely couple," Saki said.

He grinned. "Thank you, Dr. Jones."

Saki forced herself to smile back. Her son hadn't had any qualms keeping the relationship from her, but clearly Hyun-sik was happier to have things out in the open. "Let's go. We have an expedition to plan."

We did not create the Chronicle, we simply discovered it, as you did. Layer upon layer of time, a stratified record of the universe. When you visit the

Chronicle, you alter it. Your presence muddles the temporal record as surely as an archaeological dig muddles the dirt at an excavation site. In the future, human archronologists will look back on you with scorn, much as you look back on looters and tomb raiders—but we forgive you. In our early encounters, we make our own errors. How can we understand something so alien before we understand it? We act out of love, but that does not erase the harm we cause. Forgive us.

Saki spent the final hours before the expedition in a departmental meeting, arguing with Dr. Li about site selection. *When* was easy. Archronologists burrowed into the Chronicle starting at the present moment and proceeding backward through layers of time, following much the same principles as used in an archaeological dig. The spatial location was trickier to choose. M.J. had believed that the plague was alien, and if he was right, the warehouse that housed the alien artifacts would be a good starting point.

"How can you argue for anything but the colony medical center?" Li demanded. "The colonists died of a plague."

"The hospital at the present moment is unlikely to have any useful information," Saki said. The final decision was hers, but she wanted the research team to understand the rationale for her choice. "Everyone in the colony is dead, and we have their medical records up to the point of the final broadcast. The colonists suspected that the plague was alien in origin. We should start with the xenoarchaeology warehouse."

There were murmurs of agreement and disagreement from the students and post-docs.

"Didn't your lifelove work in the xenoarchaeology lab?" The question came from Annabelle Hoffman, one of Li's graduate students.

The entire room went silent.

Saki opened her mouth, then closed

it. It was information from M.J. that had led her to suggest starting at the xeno-archeaology warehouse. Would she have acted on that information if it had come from someone else? She believed that she would, but what if her love for M.J. was biasing her decisions?

"You're out of line, Hoffman." Li turned to Saki. "I apologize for Annabelle. I disagree with your choice of site, but it is inappropriate of her to make this personal. Everyone on this ship has lost someone down there."

Saki was grateful to Li for diffusing the situation. They were academic rivals, yes, but they'd grown to be friends. "Thank you."

Li nodded, then launched into a long-winded argument for the hospital as an initial site. Saki was still reeling from the personal attack. Annabelle was taking notes onto her tablet, scowling at having been rebuked. Saki hated departmental politics, hated conflict. M.J. had always been her sounding board to talk her through this kind of thing, and he was gone. Maybe she shouldn't do this. Li was a brilliant researcher. The project would be in good hands if she stepped down.

Suddenly the room went quiet. Li had finished laying out her arguments, and everyone was waiting for Saki's response.

Hyun-sik came to her rescue and systematically countered Li's arguments. He was charming and persuasive, and by the end of the meeting he had convinced the group to go along with the plan to visit the xenoarchaeology warehouse first.

Saki hoped it was the right choice.

There is no objective record of the moments in your past—you filter reality through your thoughts and perceptions. Over time, you create a memory of the memory, compounding bias upon bias, layers of self-serving rationalizations, or denial, or nostalgia. Everything becomes a story. You visit the Chronicle to study us, but what you see isn't absolute truth.

The record of our past is filtered through your minds.

The control room for the temporal projector looked like the navigation bridge of an interstellar ship. A single person could work the controls, but half the department was packed into the room—most longing for a connection to the people they'd lost, others simply eager to be a part of this historic moment, the first expedition to the dead colony of New Mars.

Saki waited with Hyun-sik in the containment cylinder, a large chamber with padded walls and floors. At twenty meters in diameter and nearly two stories high, it was the largest open area on the ship. Cameras on the ceiling recorded everything that she and Hyun-sik did. From the perspective of people staying on the ship, the expedition team would flicker, disappear briefly, and return an instant later—possibly in a different location. This was the purpose of the padded floors and walls: to cushion falls and prevent injury in the event that they returned at a slightly different altitude.

The straps of Saki's pack chafed her shoulders. She and Hyun-sik stood back to back, not moving, although stillness was not strictly necessary. The projector could transport moving objects as easily as stationary ones. As long as they weren't half inside the room and half outside of it, everything would be fine. "Ready?"

"Ready," Hyun-sik confirmed.

Over the ceiling-mounted speakers, the robotic voice of the projection system counted down from twenty. Saki forced herself to breathe.

". . . three, two, one."

Their surroundings faded to black, then brightened into the cavernous warehouse that served as artifact storage for the xenoarchaeology lab. The placement was good. Saki and Hyun-sik floated in an empty aisle. Two rows of brightly colored alien artifacts towered above them. Displacement damage from their arrival was minimal; nothing of interest was likely to be in the middle of the aisle.

Silence pressed down on them. The Chronicle recorded light but not sound, and they were like projections, there without really being there. M.J. could have explained it better. This was not her first time in the Chronicle, but the lack of sound was always unnerving. There was no ambient noise, or even her own breathing and heartbeat.

"Mark location." Saki typed her words in the air, her tiny motions barely visible but easily detected by the sensors in her gloves. Her instructions appeared in the corner of Hyun-sik's glasses. She and her student set the location on their wristbands. The projection cylinder was twenty meters in diameter, and moving beyond that area in physical space could be catastrophic upon return. The second expedition into the Chronicle had ended with the research team reappearing inside the concrete foundation of the Chronos lab.

"Location marked," Hyun-sik confirmed.

Saki studied the artifacts that surrounded her. She had no idea if they were machinery or art or some kind of alien toy. Hell, for all she knew, they might be waste products or alien carapaces. They *looked* manufactured rather than biological, though—smooth, flat-bottomed ovoids that reminded her of escape pods or maybe giant eggs.

The closest artifact on her left was about three times her height and had a base of iridescent blue, dotted with specks of red, crisscrossed with a delicate lace of green and gray and black. The base, which extended to roughly the midline of each ovoid, was uniform across all the artifacts in the warehouse. The tops, however, were all different. Several were shades of green with various amounts of brown mixed in. The one immediately to her right was topped with swirls of browns and beige and grayish-white and a red so dark it looked almost black. M.J. had been so thrilled to unearth these wondrous things.

Something about them bothered her though. She vaguely remembered M.J. describing them as blue, and while that was true of the bases—

Hyun-sik pulled off his pack.

"Wait." Saki used the micro-jets on her suit to turn and face her student. He was surrounded in a semi-translucent shimmer of silvery-white, the colors of the Chronicle all swirled together where his presence disrupted it, like the dirt of an archaeological dig all churned together. At the edges of his displacement cloud there was a delicate rainbow film, like the surface of a soap bubble, data distorted but not yet destroyed.

"Sorry," Hyun-sik messaged. "Everything looked clear in my direction."

Saki scanned the warehouse. The recording drones would have no problem collecting data on the alien artifacts. Her job was to look for anomalies, things the drones might miss or inadvertently destroy. She studied the ceiling of the warehouse.

A maintenance walkway wrapped around the building, a platform of silvery mesh suspended from the lighter silver metal of the ceiling. The walkway was higher than the two-story ceiling of the containment cylinder, outside of their priority area. On the walkway, near one of the bright ceiling lights, something looked odd. "I don't think we were the first ones here."

Hyun-sik followed her gaze. "Displacement cloud?"

"There, by the lights." Saki studied the shape on the walkway. It was hard to tell at this distance, but the displacement cloud was roughly the right size to be human. "Unfortunately we have no way to get up there for a closer look."

"I can reprogram a few of the bees—"

"Yes." It was not ideal. Drones were good at recording physical objects, but had difficulty picking up the outlines of distortion clouds and other anomalies. Moving through the Chronicle was difficult, though not impossible. It was similar to free fall in open space. Things you brought with you were solid, but everything else was basically a projection.

"It is too far for the microjets," Hyunsik continued, "but we could tie ourselves together and push off each other so that someone could have a closer look."

Saki had been considering that very option, but it was too dangerous. If something went wrong and they couldn't get back to their marks, they could reappear inside a station wall, or off the ship entirely, or in a location occupied by another person. She wanted desperately to take a closer look, because if the distortion cloud was human-shaped it meant . . . "No. It's too risky. We'll send drones."

There was nothing else that merited a more thorough investigation, so they released the recording drones, a flying army of bee-sized cameras that recorded every object from multiple angles. Seventeen drones flew to the ceiling and recorded the region of the walkway that had the distortion. Saki hoped the recording would be detailed enough to be useful. The disruption to the Chronicle was like ripples in a pond, spreading from the present into the past and future record, tiny trails of white blurring together into a jumbled cloud.

M.J. had always followed the minimalist school of archronology; he liked to observe the Chronicle from a single unobtrusive spot. He had disapproved of recording equipment, of cameras and drones. It would be so like him to stand on an observation walkway, far above the scene he wanted to observe. But this moment was in his future, a part of the Chronicle that hadn't been laid down yet when he died. There was no way for him to be here.

The drones had exhausted all the open space and started flying through objects to gather data on their internal properties. By the time the drones flew back into their transport box, the warehouse was a cloud of white with only traces of the original data.

We did not begin here. The urge to expand and grow came to us from another relationship. They came to us, and we learned their love of exploration, which eventually led us to you. It doesn't matter that we arrive here before you, we are patient, we will wait.

The reconstruction lab was crammed full of people—students and post-docs and faculty carefully combing through data from the drones on tablets, occasionally projecting data onto the wall to get a better look at the details. The 3D printer hummed, printing small-scale reproductions of the alien artifacts.

"The initial reports we received described the artifact bases, but not the tops." Li's voice rose over the general din of the room. "The artifacts *changed* sometime after the colony stopped sending reports."

Annabelle said something in response, but Saki couldn't quite make it out. She shook her head and tried to focus on the drone recordings from the seventeen drones that had flown to the ceiling to investigate the anomaly. It was a human outline, which meant that they weren't the first ones to visit that portion of the Chronicle. Saki couldn't make out the figure's features. She wasn't sure if the lack of resolution was due to the drones having difficulty recording something that wasn't technically an object, or if the person had moved enough to blur the cloud they left behind.

She wanted desperately to believe that it was M.J. An unmoving human figure was consistent with his minimalist style of research. Visiting a future Chronicle was forbidden, and only theoretically possible, but under the circumstances—

"Any luck?" Dr. Li interrupted her train of thought.

Saki shook her head. "Someone was clearly in this part of the Chronicle before us, and the outline is human. Beyond that I don't think we will get anything else from these damn drone recordings."

"Shame you couldn't get up there to get a closer look." There was a mischievous sparkle in Li's eyes when she said it, almost like it was a backwards-in-time dare, a challenge.

"Too risky," Saki said. "And we might not have gotten more than what came off the drones. If it had been just me, I might have chanced it, but I'm responsible for the safety of my student—"

"I'm only teasing," Li said softly. "Sorry. This is a hard expedition for all of us. The captain is pushing for answers and Annabelle is trying to convince anyone who will listen that we need a surface mission to look at the original artifacts."

"Foolishness. We can't even get a working probe down there, we couldn't possibly send people. Maybe the next expedition into the Chronicle will bring us more answers."

"I hope so."

Dr. Li went back to supervising the work at the 3D printer. Like M.J., her research spanned both archronology and xenoarchaeology, and her team was doing most of the artifact reconstruction and analysis. They were in a difficult position—the captain wanted answers *now* about whether the artifacts were dangerous, but something so completely alien could take years of research to decipher, if they were even knowable at all.

Someone chooses which part of our story is told. Sometimes it is you, and sometimes it is us. We repeat ourselves because we always focus on the same things, we structure our narratives in the same ways. You are no different. Some things change, but others always stay the same. Eventually our voices will blend together to create something beautiful and new. We learned anticipation before we met you, and you know it too, though you do not feel it for us.

When Saki returned to her family quarters, she messaged Kenzou. He did not respond. Off with Hyun-sik, probably. Saki ordered scotch (neat) from the replicator, and savored the burn down her throat as she sipped it. This particular scotch was one of M.J.'s creations, heavy on smoke but light on peat, with just the tiniest bit of sweetness at the end.

She played one of M.J.'s old vid letters on her tablet. He rambled cheerfully about his day, the artifacts he'd dug up at the site of the abandoned alien ruins, his plan to someday visit that part of the Chronicle with Saki so that they could see the aliens at the height of their civilization. He was trying to solve the mystery of why the aliens had left the planet—there was no trace of them, not a single scrap of organic remains. They'd had long back and forth discussions on whether the aliens were simply so biologically foreign that the remains were unrecognizable. Perhaps the city itself was the alien, or their bodies were ephemeral, or the artifacts somehow stored their remains. So many slowtime conversations, in vid letters back and forth from Earth. Then a backlog of vids that M.J. had sent while she was in stasis for the interstellar trip.

This vid was from several months before she woke, one of the last before M.J. started showing signs of the plague that wiped out the colony. Saki barely listened to the words. She lost herself in M.J.'s deep brown eyes and let the soothing sound of his voice wash over her.

"Octavia's parakeet up and died last night," M.J. said.

His words brought Saki back to the present. The parakeet reminded Saki of something from another letter, or had it been one of M.J.'s lecture transcripts? He'd said something about crops failing, first outside of the domes and later even in the greenhouses. Plants, animals, humans—everything in the colony had died. Everyone on the ship assumed that the crops and animals had died because the people of the colony had gotten too sick to tend them, but what if the plague had taken out everything?

She had to find out.

Most of M.J.'s letters she had watched many times, but there was one she'd seen only once because she couldn't bear to re-live the pain of it. The last letter. She called it up on her tablet, then drank the rest of her scotch before hitting play. M.J.'s hair was shaved to a short black stubble and his face was sallow and sunken. He was in the control room of the colony's temporal projector, working on his research right up until the end.

"They can't isolate a virus. Our im-mune systems seem to be attacking some-thing, but we have no idea what, or why, and our bodies are breaking down. How can we stop something if we can't figure out what it is?"

"I will hold on as long as I can, my life-love, but the plague is accelerating. Don't come to the surface, use the Chronicle. Whatever this is, it has to be alien."

She closed her eyes and listened to him describe the fall of the colony. If she closed her eyes and ignored the content of the words, if she forced herself not to hear the frailness in his voice, if she pushed away all the realities she could not accept—it was like he was still down there, a quick shuttle hop away, waiting for her to join him.

"The transmission systems have started to go. This alien world is harsh, and without our entire colony fighting to make it hospitable, everything is failing, all our efforts falling apart. Entropy will turn us all to dust. This will probably be my last letter, but perhaps when you arrive you will see me in the Chronicle."

"Keep fighting. Live for both of us. I love you."

"You home, Mom?" Kenzou called out as he came in. "I'm going out with Hyun-sik tonight, but . . . are you crying? What happened?"

Saki rubbed away the tears and gestured down at the tablet. "Vids. The old letters."

Kenzou hugged her. "I miss him, too, but you shouldn't watch those. You need to hold yourself together until the expeditions are done."

"I'm not going to pretend he doesn't exist."

She went to the replicator and ordered another scotch.

Kenzou picked up the dishes she'd left on the counter, clearing away her clutter probably without even realizing he was doing it. He was so like his father in some ways, and now he wanted to act as though nothing had happened.

The silence between them stretched long. He punched some commands into the replicator but nothing happened.

"He was your father," Saki said softly.

"And you think this doesn't hurt?" Kenzou snapped. He smacked the side of the replicator and it beeped and let out a hiss of steam. His fingers danced across the keypad again, hitting each button far harder than necessary. The replicator produced a cup of green tea, and his brief moment of anger passed. "I'm trying to move on. Dad would have wanted that."

The outburst made her want to hold him like she had when he was young. She'd buried herself in her work these last few months, and he had found his comfort elsewhere. He'd finished growing up sometime when she wasn't looking.

"I'm sorry," she said. "Go, spend time with your boyfriend."

He softened. "You shouldn't drink alone, Mom."

"And you shouldn't secretly date my students," she scolded gently. "It's very awkward when the whole lab knows who my son is dating before I do!"

He sipped his tea. "There aren't that many people on station, word has a way of getting around."

After a short pause he added, "You could ask Dr. Li to have a drink with you, if you insist on drinking."

"I don't think she would . . ." Saki shook her head.

"And that's why your entire lab knows these things before you do." He finished his tea, then washed the cup and put it away. "You don't notice what is right in front of you."

"I'm not ready to move on." She looked down at the menu on her tablet, the list of recently viewed vids a line of tiny icons of M.J.'s face. He was supposed to be here, waiting for her. They were supposed to have such a wonderful life.

"I know." He hugged her. "But I think you can get there."

Layers of information diminish as they recede from the original source. In archaeology, you remove the artifacts from their context, change a physical record into descriptions and photographs. You choose what gets recorded, often unaware of what you do not think to keep. Your impressions—logged in books or electroni-

*cally on tablets or in whatever medium
is currently in fashion—are themselves
a physical record that future researchers
might find, when you are dead and gone.*

Saki was with Li in the Chronicle, four
weeks after the collapse.

The third floor of the hospital was
empty. Not just devoid of people—this
was a part of the Chronicle that came after
everyone had died, so that wasn't surpris-
ing. The place was half cleaned out. Foam
mattresses on metal frames, but someone
or something had taken the sheets. Nothing
in the planters, not even dry dead plants.
This wasn't long after the collapse, and the
pieces simply did not fit.

"Why would anyone bother taking
things from the hospital while everyone
was dying?" Li messaged. "And why are
there no bodies? There was no one left at
the end to take care of the remains."

The crops had failed, the parrot had
died, the hospital was empty. Saki knew

there had to be a connection, but what was it? She scanned the area for clues. In a patch of bright sunlight near one of the windows, she saw the faint outline of a distortion, another visitor to the Chronicle. The window was at the edge of the containment area, but probably within reach.

"Someone else was here," Saki typed, "by that window."

"I think you're right. Closer look?" Li fished out the rope from her pack. "I'm not a graduate student, so you're not responsible for my wellbeing."

Saki caught herself before explaining that as lead researcher she was still responsible for the welfare of everyone on the team. Li was partly teasing, but it held some truth, too. If Li was willing to risk it, they could investigate.

"Can I be the one to go?" Saki asked.

"You think it might be M.J." Li did not phrase it as a question.

"Yes."

Li fastened the rope securely around

her waist and handed Saki the other end. They checked each other's knots, then checked them again. If they came untied, it would be difficult or maybe impossible to get back to their marks. They spun themselves around and pressed their palms and feet together. "Gently. We can try again if you don't get far enough."

Li's hands were smaller than her own, and warm.

"Ready?"

Saki felt the tiny movements of Li's fingers as she typed the word. She nodded. "Three, two, one."

They pushed off of each other, propelling Saki towards the window and Li in the opposite direction, leaving a wide white scar across the Chronicle between them. Saki managed to contort her body around so that she could see where she was going as she drifted towards the window. The human form that stood there was not facing the hospital, and she couldn't see their face. She reached the end of the rope a meter short of the window.

"Is it M.J.?" Li messaged from across the room.

"I don't know," Saki replied.

The white figure by the window was about the right height to be M.J., about the right shape. But the colony was huge, and even narrowed down to just the archronologists, it could have been any number of people. Saki twisted around to gain a few more centimeters, but she couldn't see well enough to know one way or the other. If she untied the rope and used the micro-jets on her suit—but no, that would leave Li stranded.

"Whoever it is, they were looking out the window." Saki tore her gaze away from the figure that might or might not be her lifelove. She'd seen the New Mars campus many times, even this part of campus, because the hospital was across the quad from the archronology building. M.J. had sometimes recorded his vid letters there, on the yellow-tinged grass that grew beneath the terrafruit trees.

Outside the window, there were no

trees. There was no grass. Not even dry brown grass and dead leafless trees. It was bare ground. Nothing but a layer of red New Martian dust.

"All of it is gone," Saki typed. "Every living thing was destroyed."

No one had noticed it in the warehouse because they'd had no reason to expect any living things to be there.

She and Li pulled themselves back to the center of the room, climbing their rope hand over hand until they were back at their marks. They adjusted the programming of their bees in hopes that they could get a clear image of the other visitor to the record, and set them swarming around the room.

"It's more than that," Li messaged as the bees catalogued the room. "That's why this room is so odd. Everything organic is gone. Whatever is left is all metal or plastic."

It was obvious as soon as she said it, but something still didn't fit. "The alien artifacts, back in the warehouse—those were made from organic materials. Why weren't they destroyed with everything else?"

One of our beloveds believes that all important things are infinite. Numbers. Time. Love. They think that the infinite should never be seen. We erase vast sections of the Chronicle out of love, but this infuriates some of our other beloveds. To embrace so many different loves, scattered across the galaxy, is difficult to navigate. It is not possible to please everyone.

Saki stood back to back with Hyun-sik. Their surroundings shifted from gray to orange-red. The two of them were floating beneath the open sky in a carefully excavated pit. The dig site was laid out in a grid, black cords stretched between stakes, claylike soil removed layer by layer and carefully analyzed. Fine red dust swirled in an eerily silent wind and gathered in the corners of the pit.

Hyun-sik swayed on his feet.

"The Chronicle is an image, being here is no different from being in an enclosed warehouse," Saki reminded him. He looked ill, and if he threw up in the Chronicle it might obscure important data. Even if it didn't, it would definitely be unpleasant.

"I've never been outside. It is big and open and being weightless here feels wrong," Hyun-sik messaged. He took a deep breath. "And the dust is moving."

"Human consciousness is tied to the passage of time. In an abandoned indoor environment like the warehouse, there are long stretches of time where nothing moves or changes. It feels like a single moment in time. But we are viewing moving sections of the record, which is why we try to spend as little time here as we can," Saki answered.

"Sorry." He still looked a little green, but he managed not to vomit. Saki turned her attention back to their surroundings. There were no visible distortions here, no intrusions into the time record. M.J. hadn't visited the Chronicle of this time and place.

At Li's insistence, the team had done a three-day drone sweep of the entire colony starting at the moment of the last known transmission. Wiping out so much of the Chronicle felt incredibly wasteful, especially for such an important historic moment. If some future research team came to study the planet, all they'd find of those final days was a sea of white, the destruction inherent in collecting the data. Though if Saki was honest, the thing that bothered her most was that she couldn't be there for M.J.'s final moments. They had burrowed into the Chronicle deeper than his death, deeper than his final acts, leaving broad swaths of destruction in their wake.

He was gone, why should it matter what happened to the Chronicle of his life? But it felt like deleting his letters, or erasing him from the list of contacts on her tablet.

She tried to focus on the present. This site was a few weeks before the final transmission. They were here to gather information about the alien artifacts in situ.

Perhaps they could notice something that M.J. and his team had missed.

In the distance, the nearest colony dome glimmered in the sun, sitting on the surface like a soap bubble. There were people living inside the dome—M.J. was there, working or sleeping or recording a vid letter that she would not read until months later. So many people, and all of them would soon be dead. Were already dead, outside the Chronicle. Colonies were so fragile, like the bubbles they resembled. The domes themselves were reasonably sturdy, but the life inside . . . New Mars was not the first failed colony, and it would not be the last.

The sun was bright but not hot. Expeditions into the Chronicle were an odd limbo, real but not real, like watching a vid from the inside.

"That one looks unfinished," Hyun-sik messaged, pointing to a partially exposed artifact. It was an iridescent blue, like the bases of the artifacts in the warehouse, but the upper surface of the artifact did not have the smoothly curved edges that were universal to everything they'd seen so far.

"They changed so quickly," Saki mused. She'd read M.J.'s descriptions of the artifacts, and looked at the images of them, but there was something more powerful about seeing one full scale here in the Chronicle. "And right as the colony collapsed. The two things must be related."

She shuddered, remembering the drone vids of the final collapse. After weeks of slow progression, everything in the colony started dying. She'd forced herself to watch a clip from the hospital—dozens of colonists filling the beds, tended by medics who eventually collapsed wherever they were standing. Everyone dead within minutes of each other, and then—Saki squeezed her eyes shut tight as though it would ward off the memory—the bodies disintegrated. Flesh, bone, blood, clothes, everything organic broke down into a fine dust that swirled in the breeze of the ventilation systems.

She opened her eyes to the swirling red dust of the excavation site, suddenly feeling every bit as ill as Hyun-sik looked. Such a terrible way to die and there was nothing left. No bodies to cremate, no bones to bury. It was as if the entire colony had never existed, and M.J. had died down here and that entire moment was nothing but a sea of drone-distortion white.

"Are you okay, Dr. Jones?" Hyun-sik messaged.

"Sorry," she answered. "Did you watch the drone-vids from the collapse?"

He nodded, and his face went pale. "Only a little. Worse than the most terrible nightmare, and yet real."

Saki focused all her attention on the artifact half-buried in the red dirt, forcing everything else out of her mind. She searched the blue for any trace of other colors, but there was nothing else there. "I don't know how the artifacts changed so quickly, or why. Maybe Dr. Li can figure it out from the recordings."

"Release the drones?" Hyun-sik asked.

"Wait." Saki pointed toward the colony dome, her arm wiping away a small section of the Chronicle as she moved. "Look."

Clouds of red dust rose up from the ground, far away and hard to see.

"Dust storm?" Hyun-sik turned his head slightly, trying to disturb the record as little as possible.

"Jeeps." Saki stared at the approaching clouds of dust, rising from vehicles too distant to see. M.J. might be in one of them, making the trek over rough terrain to get to the dig site. Saki tried to remember how far the dig site was from the dome— forty kilometers? Maybe fifty? The dig site was on a small hill, and Saki couldn't quite remember the math for calculating distance to the horizon. It was estimates stacked on estimates, and although she desperately wanted to see M.J., her conclusion was the same no matter how she ran the calculation—they couldn't wait for the slow-moving jeeps to arrive.

"Do you see anything else that merits a closer look?" Saki typed.

Hyun-sik stared at the approaching jeeps. "If we had come a couple hours later, there would have been people here."

"Yes."

It wasn't M.J., Saki reminded herself, only an echo. Her lifelove wasn't really here. Saki had Hyun-sik release the drones and soon they were surrounded by white, much as the jeeps were enveloped in a cloud of red.

The drones finished, and the jeeps were still far in the distance. M.J. always did drive damnably slow. Saki waved goodbye to jeeps that couldn't see her. When they blinked back into the projection room, she was visibly shaken. Hyun-sik politely invited her to join him and Kenzou for dinner, but that would be awkward at best and she didn't have the energy to make conversation. Saki kept it together long enough to get back to her quarters.

Safely behind closed doors, she called up the vid letter that M.J. had sent around the time she'd just visited. He was supposed to wait for her, only a few more months. She'd been so close. The vid played in the background while she cried.

We had a physical form, once. Wings and scales and oh so many legs, everything in iridescent blue. Each time we encounter a new love, it becomes a part of who we are. No, we do not blend our loves into one single entity—the core of us would be lost against such vastness. We always remain half ourselves, a collective of individuals, a society of linked minds. How could we exclude you from such a union?

The captain sent probes to the surface that were entirely inorganic—no synthetic rubber seals or carbon-based fuels—and this time the probes did not fail. They found nanites in the dust. Visits to the Chronicle were downgraded in priority as other teams worked to neutralize the alien technology. Saki tried to stay focused on her research, but without the urgency and tight deadlines, she found herself drawn into the past. She watched letters from M.J. in a long chain, one vid after the next. The hard ones, the sad ones, everything she'd been avoiding so that she could be functional enough to do research.

The last vid-letter from M.J. was recorded not in his office but in the control room for the temporal projector. Saki had asked about it at the time, and he'd explained that he had one last trip to make, and the colony was running out of time. She'd watched it twice now, and M.J. looked so frail. But there was something Saki had to check. A hunch.

For the first half of the vid, M.J. sat near enough to the camera to fill nearly the entire field of view. He thought the plague was accelerating, becoming increasingly deadly. He talked about the people who had died and the people who were still dying, switching erratically between cold clinical assessment and tearful reminiscence. Saki cried right along with her lost love, harsh ugly tears that blurred her vision so badly that she nearly missed what she was looking for.

She paused and rewound. There, in the middle of the video, M.J. had gotten up to make an adjustment to the controls. The camera should have stayed with him, but for a brief moment it recorded the settings of the projector. The point in the record where M.J. was going.

Saki wrote down the coordinates of space and time. It was on New Mars, of course. It was also in the future. She studied the other settings on the projector, noting the changes he'd made to accommodate projection in the wrong direction.

M.J. had visited a future Chronicle, and left her the clues she needed to follow him.

She set her com status to do not disturb, and marked the temporal projector as undergoing maintenance. There was no way she could make it through a vid recording without falling apart, so she wrote old-fashioned letters to Kenzou, to her graduate students, to Li—just in case something went wrong.

When she stepped out into the corridor, Hyun-sik and Kenzou were there.

She froze.

"I will work the controls for you, Dr. Jones," Hyun-sik said. "It is safer than programming them on a delay."

"How did you—?"

"You love him, you can't let him go," Kenzou said. "You've always been terrible at goodbyes. You want to see as much of his time on the colonies as possible, and there's no way to get approval for most of it."

"Also, marking the temporal projector as 'scheduled maintenance' when our temporal engineer is in the middle of their sleep cycle won't fool anyone who is actually paying attention to the schedule," Hyun-sik added.

"Thinking of making an unauthorized trip yourself?" Saki asked, raising an eyebrow at her student.

"Come on," Hyun-sik didn't answer her question. "It won't be long before someone else notices."

They went to the control room, and
Saki adjusted the settings and wiring to
match what she'd seen in M.J.'s vid. The
two young men sat together and watched
her work, Kenzou resting his head on
Hyun-sik's shoulder.

When she'd finished, Hyun-sik came
to examine the controls. "That is twenty
years from now."

"Yes."

"No one has visited a future Chronicle
before. It is forbidden by the IRB and the
theory is completely untested."

"It worked for M.J.," Saki said softly.
She didn't have absolute proof that those
distortion clouds in the Chronicle had been
him, but who else could it be? No other
humans had been here since the collapse,
and whoever it was had selected expedition sites that she was likely to visit. M.J.
was showing her that he had successfully
visited the future. He wanted her to meet
him at those last coordinates.

"Of course it did," Kenzou said, chuck-
ling. "He was so damn brilliant."

Saki wanted to laugh with him, but all she managed was a pained smile. "And so are you. You'll get into trouble for this. It could damage your careers."

"If we weren't here, would you bother to come back?"

Saki blushed, thinking of the letters she'd left in her quarters, just in case. M.J. had gone to some recorded moment of future. Maybe he had stayed there. This was a way to be with him, outside of time and space. If she came back, she would have to face the consequences of making an unauthorized trip. It was not so farfetched to think that she might stay in the Chronicle.

"Now you have a reason to return," Hyun-sik said. "Otherwise Kenzou and I will have to face whatever consequences come of this trip alone."

Saki sighed. They knew her too well. She couldn't stay in the Chronicle and throw them to the fates. "I promise to return."

This is a love story, but it does not end with happily ever after. It doesn't end at all. Your stories are always so rigidly shaped—beginning, middle, end. There are strands of love in your narratives, all neat and tidy in the chaos of reality. Our love is scattered across time and space, without order, without endings.

Visiting the Chronicle in the past was like watching a series of moments in time, but the future held uncertainty. Saki split into a million selves, all separate but tied together by a fragile strand of consciousness, anchored to a single moment but fanning out into possibilities.

She was at the site of the xenoarchaeology warehouse, mostly.

Smaller infinities of herself remained in the control room due to projector malfunction or a last minute change of heart. In other realities, the warehouse had been relocated, or destroyed, or rebuilt into alien architectures her mind couldn't fully grasp. She was casting a net of white into the future, disturbing the fabric of the Chronicle before it was even laid down.

Saki focused on the largest set of her infinities, the fraction of herself on New Mars, inside the warehouse and surrounded by alien artifacts. The most probable futures, the ones with the least variation.

M.J. was there, surrounded by a bubble of white where he had disrupted the Chronicle.

Saki focused her attention further, to a single future where they had calibrated their coms through trial and error or intuition or perhaps purely by chance. There was no sound in the Chronicle, but they could communicate.

"Hello, my lifelove," M.J. messaged.

"I can't believe it's really you," Saki answered. "I missed you so much."

"Me too. I worried that I'd never see you again." He gestured to the artifacts. "Did you solve it?"

She nodded. "Nanites. The bases of

the artifacts generate nanites, and clouds of them mix with the dust. They consumed everything organic to build the tops of the artifacts."

"Yes. Everything was buried at first, and the nanites were accustomed to a different kind of organic matter," M.J. typed. "But they adapted, and they multiplied."

Saki shuddered. "Why would they make something so terrible?"

"Ah. Like me, you only got part of it." He gestured at the artifacts that surrounded them. "The iridescent blue on the bottom are the aliens, or a physical shell of them, anyway. The nanites are the way they make connections, transforming other species they encounter into something they themselves can understand."

"Why didn't you explain this in your reports?"

"The pieces were there, but I didn't put it all together until I got to the futures." He gestured at the warehouse around them with one arm, careful to stay within his already distorted bubble of white.

In this future, she and M.J. were alone, but in many of the others the warehouse was crowded with people. Saki recognized passengers and crew from the ship. They walked among the artifacts with an almost religious air, most of them pausing near one particular artifact, reaching out to touch it.

She sifted through the other futures and found the common threads. The worship of the artifacts, the people of the station living down on the colony, untouched by the nanites. "I don't understand what happened."

"Once the aliens realized what they were doing to us, they stopped. They had absorbed our crops, our trees, our pets. Each species into its own artifact." He turned to face the closest artifact, the one that she'd seen so many people focus their attentions on in parallel futures. "This one holds all the human colonists."

"They are visiting their loved ones, worshipping their ancestors."

"Yes."

"I will come here to visit you." Saki could see it in the futures. "I was so angry when Li sent drones to record the final moments of the colony. I should have been there to look for you, but that's a biased reason, too wrong to even mention in a departmental meeting. I couldn't find you in the drone vids, but there was so much data. Everyone and everything dead, and then systematically taken apart by the nanites. Everyone."

"It is what taught the aliens to let the rest of humankind go."

"They didn't learn! They took all the organics from the probes we sent."

"New tech, right? Synthetic organics that weren't in use on the colonies, that the nanites didn't recognize. You can see the futures, Saki. The colony is absorbed into the artifacts, but at least we save everyone else."

"We? You can't go back there. I don't want to visit an alien shrine of you, I want to stay. I want *us* to stay." Saki flailed her arms helplessly, then stared down at her wristband. "I promised Kenzou that I would go back."

"You have a future to create," M.J. answered. "Tell Kenzou that I love him. His futures are beautiful."

"I could save you somehow. Save everyone." Saki studied the artifacts. "Or I could stay. It doesn't matter how long I'm here, in the projection room we only flicker for an instant—"

"I came here to wait for you." M.J. smiled sadly. "Now we've had our moment, and I should return to my own time. Go first, my lifelove, so that you don't have to watch me leave. Live for both of us."

It was foolish, futile, but Saki reached out to M.J., blurring the Chronicle to white between them. He mirrored her movement, bringing his fingertips to hers. For a moment she thought that they would touch, but coming from such different times, using different projectors—they weren't quite in sync. His fingertips blurred to white.

She pulled her hand back to her chest,

holding it to her heart. She couldn't bring herself to type goodbye. Instead she did her best to smile through her tears. "I'll keep studying the alien civilization, like we dreamed."

He returned her smile, and his eyes were as wet with tears as her own. Before she lost the will to do it, she slapped the button on her wristband. Only then, as she was leaving, did he send his last message, "Goodbye, my lifelove."

All her selves in all the infinite possible futures collapsed into a single Saki, and she was back in the projection room, tears streaming down her face.

We know you better now. We love you enough to leave you alone.

Saki pulled off her gloves and touched the cool surface of the alien artifact. M.J. was part of this object. All the colonists were. Those first colonists who had lost their lives to make the aliens understand that humankind didn't want to be forcibly absorbed. Was M.J.'s consciousness still there, a part of something bigger? Saki liked to think so.

With her palm pressed against the artifact, she closed her eyes and focused. They were learning to communicate, slowly over time. It was telling her a story. One side of the story, and the other side was hers.

She knew that she was biased, that her version of reality would be hopelessly flawed and imperfect. That she would not even realize all the things she would not think to write, but she recorded both sides of the story as best she could.

This is a love story, the last of a series of moments when we meet.

FLOWERS IN
THE CHRONICLE

<Probably it is a supernova, nothing to worry about.>

<No, this is different. It keeps getting worse. I am losing moments. I have fought this disease before. A sickness that spreads from a single point within my time and space.>

S aki studied the data from her latest research project. Even after all these years, no one knew how the Chronicle was formed—they simply accepted that it was a visual echo of the universe and used it to peer through time. The field of archronology continued to grow, and people became ever greedier for the treasure trove of knowledge that was buried in the layers of time. But something had changed. The amount of energy needed to make an expedition into the Chronicle had always been stable, and suddenly last month it skyrocketed.

Hyun-sik was developing a work-around to decrease the energy cost, but Saki was determined to solve the underlying mystery. She'd retired from venturing into the Chronicle herself, but that didn't stop her from gathering reports from other expeditions. Humans were exploring the Chronicle, starting from the present moment and blooming ever outward like a flower with delicate petals of white. It was human nature to expand—to fill the planet, to spread through space, to explore the past—and every moment of the Chronicle they visited, they destroyed.

"It's late, you should go home," Hyun-sik said quietly from the doorway.

"She won't be there, so why should I bother?" Saki said, her voice harsher than she meant for it to be. "Besides, this work is important, I need to finish it before—"

Before the treatments stopped working, before rogue alien nanites turned her brain into a tangle of scars. She'd heard rumors that researchers were closing in on a cure, but unless it was ready for testing soon, it'd be too late for Saki.

"Come have dinner with me and Kenzou if you don't want to go home," Hyunsik said patiently. After a long pause he added, "Yingtai went to the outer moons to pursue her work. Would you have wanted her to do otherwise simply to be in the same physical space? It is only for a few more months."

Saki hadn't been diagnosed with nanite-induced cognitive degeneration when Yingtai left, but even if they'd known . . . Saki shook her head. It hurt too much to talk about, so instead she turned her attention back to her work.

"Our expeditions through the Chronicle are like a chrysanthemum," Saki mused. She adjusted the scale until all of known space fit on a single screen. "And here is the combined data for all the other alien species we've encountered."

She ran her simulation at high speed and tiny bursts of white destruction appeared everywhere, like a meadow of flowers blooming in spring.

<Are you getting treatment?>
<Yes.>
<That spot is still growing. It is start-ing to merge with some of the others.>
<Yes. But the growth is slower with treatment.>
<You know that there is a cure.>
<I am hoping it will stop on its own. I hate the cure. I hate what it means.>
<You are too sentimental.>
<Yes.>

Saki sat on the rust-orange couch that Hyun-sik and her son had picked out for their living room. She hated the color. It reminded her too much of New Mars.

"Mom?" Kenzou called out from the kitchen. "Dinner's ready."

"I'm waiting for Yingtai," Saki said. "She's late."

Kenzou frowned. "She's on a research expedition, remember? Did you take your meds?"

"I was so focused on work I guess I forgot." That was bad. There were tangles of scar tissue in her brain, like vines choking away her thoughts, blooming with tiny flowers. No, that was something else. The flowers were in the Chronicle. She was closing in on something important in her data, but it eluded her, slipped away through the ever-growing gaps in her brain.

Flowers in the Chronicle, tangles in her brain. Meds.

Kenzou handed her some pills. "You have to take them regularly. Maybe set an alarm?"

She took the pills and swallowed them dry.

"They're developing a cure," Kenzou said. "A way to target these new nanites using a modified version of the old ones that were responsible for the plague."

"Fighting a new disease with the old plague sounds risky. Much as I still miss M.J., I don't want to join him in those alien eggs."

"Some people think of these medical

advances as a form of reparations," Ken-zou said. "You know better than anyone that the New Martians acted out of love. They want to make it up to us. They just need volunteers."

<This version of the cure is very effective.>

<Do I have to do it now?>

<The earlier you cure the disease, the more moments you will retain.>

<Yes. But I always hope that they will learn.>

After several days of taking her medication consistently, Saki felt more like herself. She combed through her data, staring at the bouquet of blossoms where the Chronicle had been wiped away. "They never bloom beyond a certain size."

She hurried down the hall to Hyun-sik's office. "There's a maximum volume to the disruptions. No known species has exceeded a fixed amount of damage to the Chronicle."

Hyun-sik paused to consider this. "Species stop causing damage at a certain point? Gain technology that allows them to explore the Chronicle without harming it?"

Saki shook her head. "What if the nanites I'm fighting against are sentient?"

"What?" Hyun-sik asked. "Did you forget your meds today?"

"No. Listen. What if . . ." Saki flailed her hands, trying to explain. "What if we—all the species that have damaged the Chronicle—are a disease, and the Chronicle can preserve itself by slowing our spread? What if there is a *treatment.* We're nearing the point of no return, the point where every other species either withdrew from the Chronicle or was locked out."

"Or was wiped out," Hyun-sik said.

"A cure." Saki shuddered. "There are only two projectors, one here and one on Earth. If we can shut them both down, we might be safe."

"Getting individuals to act for the greater good has always been difficult. Earth was almost destroyed several times before we managed to establish ourselves beyond it. If we hadn't stumbled onto the aliens on New Mars, we might not have learned to be quiet enough to avoid the predatory species that roam our regions of space. The forest is dark for a reason. Maybe the Chronicle must also go dark."

"If a virus kills its host too fast, it will die before it can spread," Saki said. Did the Chronicle know that the blossoms of destruction were caused by sentient beings? Did it care? Should it care? The rogue alien nanites Saki was fighting weren't believed to be sentient, but if the tangles in her brain were the architecture of some microscopic civilization, would she decline a cure and sacrifice her mind for theirs?

"History is full of tipping points, crises," Hyun-sik agreed. "And so far we have picked the path that keeps us in existence."

He called up a screen of notes and stared at the lines of text. "I'll destroy my research on how to sidestep the increased energy demands. That will buy us time to try and end the expeditions entirely. Hopefully it will be enough."

Saki nodded. It would be a terrible blow to Hyun-sik's career, but they had to do everything they could to not harm their host.

Her wristband alarm chirped. Hyun-sik passed her a glass of water and her bottle of medication. It would keep the nanites at bay, at least long enough that her mind would still be intact when Yingtai returned. A treatment, not a cure.

She took her pills.

AUTHOR NOTES

In "The Archronology of Love," the main idea I wanted to explore was the nature of archaeology—the way a dig site is destroyed by the process of gathering information. We trade real-world objects in their physical context for records, photographs, carbon dating, and/or other data. The process is obviously different, but conceptually archaeology and archronology remind me of quantum mechanics, where observation collapses the wave function.

The novelette draws from bits and pieces of inspiration across a long period of time, starting with an archaeological dig I did as an undergraduate in 1999. Other elements draw on more recent experiences—missing a loved one, the campus quad at University of Washington. The bases of the alien artifacts in the novelette were inspired by an iridescent blue beetle I saw on a trip to Japan. I find it interesting the different images and moments that stay with me over time and get mashed together into stories.

One disadvantage to having a writing process that begins with a mishmash of ideas is that I find it difficult to write new stories in a preexisting world—I don't do well if I try to 'follow the characters' and see what they do after the story ends. Instead I need to come up with a new set of ideas to explore. For the flash story "Flowers in the Chronicle," I wanted to play with ideas of disease, tipping points, and individual gain vs. the greater good.

ABOUT THE AUTHOR

Caroline M. Yoachim is a prolific author of short stories, appearing in *Asimov's*, *Fantasy & Science Fiction*, *Uncanny*, *Beneath Ceaseless Skies*, *Clarkesworld*, and *Lightspeed*, among other places. She has been a finalist for the Hugo, World Fantasy, Locus, and multiple Nebula Awards. Yoachim's debut short story collection, *Seven Wonders of a Once and Future World & Other Stories*, came out with Fairwood Press in 2016.